Catherine McNamara understa
ture of a tale. These structura
significant ground as one conse
into the next, and conflicts m
characters wrestle through tl
while lust, violence, and repulsion simmer in the midst of ro-
mance, sensuality, and intimacy. *Love Stories for Hectic People*
is that rare thing – a book that gets better with each rereading.
—Michael Loveday, *Three Men on the Edge*

Catherine McNamara is one of the best writers I've read in all
the time I've been in publishing. She can do more in two hundred words than most writers can do in two hundred pages.
By turns real, funny, dark, magic, ugly, and beautiful. This collection rocks.
—Christopher James, *Jellyfish Review*

Seductive love, evaporating love and sometimes 'increasingly
superb' love: it's all in these pages. Sharp, witty and deeply
real, these small stories reveal moments of connections, and
sometimes dissolution. One can't help but be captivated by
these many and varied truths, as examined by Catherine
McNamara – and the conclusion, despite the darkness, that
'Love Is an Infinite Victory'.
—Michelle Elvy, *the everrumble*

Sometimes quiet and reflective, sometimes sensual and visceral, these thirty-three stories are assured meditations on the
foibles and complexities of love – the making and unmaking of
it. This collection drifts across continents and cultures, slowly
unbuttoning aspects of relationships between an eclectic cast
of characters, and the places they find themselves.
—K.M. Elkes, *All That Is Between Us*

In *Love Stories for Hectic People*, love crosses borders with ease when another country is often a short flight away. Other borders are eased too, of age, of colour and creed. Catherine McNamara's small, succulent stories show us that love has 'urges belonging to a wider carnal history'. In these stories, you can taste this love, feel its texture, touch its skin, smell its odour and see its shimmer as it deals with absence, infidelity, danger and death. Such love, by its very nature, often hides a deep intimacy that cannot be acknowledged in public. Such love, by its very nature, is 'raw, scented and occasionally violent'; it's *hectic*.

—Abha Iyengar, *Many Fish to Fry*

A touching and contemporary collection from a gifted storyteller.

—Eric Akoto, Editor in Chief, *Litro*

A maestro of the flash form, each word lands on the page with surgical precision, and we are at once transported to a sensuous realm of intimacy and desire.

—Lana Citron, *Edible Pleasures*

Catherine McNamara is proficient in the language of sensuality, at drawing into relief all that is tacit within matters of the heart. These remarkable narratives do that boldly and with a distinctive acumen, and grace. Stories which glint with loss and allure, with touch and toxicity, from deep within the shadowlands of intimacy where certainty no longer lives.

—Rachael Smart, *smartlitreview*

LOVE STORIES FOR HECTIC PEOPLE

Catherine McNamara grew up in Sydney, ran away to Paris to write, and ended up in Ghana co-running a bar. On the way she lived in Milan, Mogadishu and Brussels, working as a translator, graphic designer, teacher, art gallery director, shoe model, mother. *The Cartography of Others* was a finalist in the People's Book Prize (UK) and won the Eyelands International Fiction Award (Greece). *Pelt and Other Stories* was a semi-finalist in the Hudson Prize (USA) and longlisted for the Frank O'Connor Award (Ireland). Her short fiction has been Pushcart-nominated and published widely. Catherine lives in a farmhouse in northern Italy.

ALSO BY CATHERINE MCNAMARA

*The Cartography of Others*
*Pelt and Other Stories*

# Love Stories
# for
# Hectic People

## Catherine McNamara

REFLEX PRESS

First published as a collection in 2021 by Reflex Press
Abingdon, Oxfordshire, OX14 3SY
www.reflex.press

ISBN: 978-1-9161115-4-7

1 3 5 7 9 10 8 6 4 2

Printed and bound in Great Britain
by Imprint Digital.

Cover image © Giacomo Piussi
Cover art work by Daniele Francesco Fona

www.reflex.press/love-stories-for-hectic-people/

*per D, con amore*

*But of our dalliance no more signs there are,*
*Than fishes leave in streams, or birds in air;*
*And between us all sweetness may be had,*
*All, all that nature yields, or art can add.*

—John Donne
Letters to Several Personages – Sappho to Philaenis

# CONTENTS

## As Simple As Water

Vasilis K and Marj B are embracing at an Athens train station (it is Ambelokipi) when Vasilis feels Marj's legs fold under her and sees her eyes roll back, and the woman he has made love to in a hotel room far above and with whom he argued (he knows he was being unjust) falls in a dead faint at his feet as the airport train rolls in on screaming rails.

A woman in a suit rushes out of the opening doors and loosens Marj's scarf and tight jeans (he sees her white belly) and checks her airways, laying her in a recovery position on the stone slabs of the train station floor.

A minute ago Marj's tongue had been enwrapping his own, and her eyes with their long grey curlicues had spoken of wanting while his had (Marj said) been wearing their dark shields, which was what she called his retracting each time before her uncomfortable fading away on public transport, taxis and planes.

Vasilis thinks now Marj will miss her plane and what will he do with her. Vasilis's day is lined up, as hers was too in another country a short flight away, and now she is lying on the station floor with a woman crouched at her side.

The seams of the woman's pants stretch over her hips. Vasilis who has been making love to Marj most of the night (except when she wept in a corner of the bed and he waited) wonders about the pelvic cavern of all women which is filled with jostling organs and squelching tubes and lengthy orifices like vivid botanical sections drawn into slithering life. He wonders whether this woman too has mauve toenails within her brown boots.

'Who is she?' The wide woman turns back and asks. Marj's small suitcase stands by the station wall.

'I don't know. I saw her fall down.' Vasilis who had not known these words would come from his mouth stares at Marj's pearly face on the ground as another train releases startled passengers who funnel away until he and the crouching woman and Marj's body are all but alone.

*

The doctor comes out and he has black hair with dandruff captured at its roots. Vasilis feels a charge of sadness to think of the doctor raising Marj's wrist and laying it by her side, lifting her eyelids and shocking each pupil with a flashlight. Vasilis still has Marj's saliva in his mouth and some (she is a vigorous kisser) has dried on his cheek and neck.

'We're doing preliminary tests,' the doctor says. 'She may have simply hit her head, or it could be some pre-existing condition. Or even the early stages of pregnancy. We may have to keep your wife here overnight.'

'I see.' Vasilis's heart is in stiff points under his skin, barred in his rib cage.

The young doctor with dirty hair stands there, looking at the language on Vasilis's face. Then he turns back to his patient, slouching up the hall with its seam of lights.

Vasilis walks outside up a concrete path and he calls his wife who would just be opening the shop on the island, and his son who has an anthropology exam in the afternoon. There had been a way to loving Marj as there is a way to loving all women, but in Marj's case it was a silken rope, a water snake with a ribboning tail, and at dawn they had been clasped at the

14

hotel window (Marj's cheeks were dry) staring out over the flushed city and now Marj is in a bed under lights and Vasilis is walking, walking.

## Foundation Song

He describes the persimmon tree as an equilibrium of weight and colour; a tree Gauguin would have liked. They stand at the bottom of her wrangled garden. The wet branches are clotted with scathing orange balls you could plunge a finger into and it would come out sullied with orange jelly, like you were poking inside breasts.

In her language the fruit is called *caco*. There is no path between the two words.

They go to a concert which is *King Arthur* by Purcell. When the King dies in the snow she can feel the capitulation of the army of her cells and the oozing inertness of her body.

After the concert he collects their coats. His phone rings and he stands on the ruffled carpet of the auditorium with his phone cupped to his ear.

In the car he tells her that his son has a disease and he will fly back to his country tomorrow. The disease is in its early stages and curable. He says he will stay there as long as it takes the boy to fight this malady.

How she misses him already. It's like a tourniquet applied to thrusts of blood.

# Genitalia

Her periods are messy. They have just moved in together and each month, at the height of her flow when the plump moon beams on their mattress, she groans with her cramps and they awaken in the morning adhered by red wounds. She heads off to the bathroom with butterfly stains on her knickers, then returns with a warm cloth to diligently wash his pink penis which has a metallic aroma.

He asks her if there is some way it can stop. Not her menstruation – of course not! – but the excessive blood loss – surely she must be anaemic – and then there is the battle-ground of their mattress. Would it not be possible to use wider pads. Or stockier tampons?

She stands up and there is a dribble down the inside of her leg.

She tells him that once, in a hotel room in Budapest, encouraged by a man she loved as a student, she painted a line of hieroglyphics (she is an Egyptologist) on the yellow wall.

He asks her does she not feel guilty about that? The woman who had to clean her *blood*? His parents are people with menial jobs.

She tells him that for sure the hotel has been bulldozed down by now and the piece of mortar she painted would be lying in a pile of rubble along the river. Where it gleams at night.

'Be serious,' he says.

She tells him that when women are pregnant they do not menstruate for nine months, and often when the mother breastfeeds, also, her periods do not return. She has a New Age older sister who breastfed for three years and did not shed blood in nearly four.

He feels very ignorant. His parents were anatomically contained and he did not know this.

*

Now his girlfriend is pregnant. The full moon dances across their bed and the mattress has been turned, and he proudly watches the drum of her belly when she sleeps and the flicker of an elbow or ankle of his own son revolving within. There is no blood, no washing of his pink genitals or splattering of hers, no sense that they are compelled by the Earth to be.

## *The Woman Whose Husband Died in a Climbing Accident*

Helga Pfenning lost her husband, Jan, in an accident on Aconcagua. His companions told her Jan had been fretful and disoriented when they bedded down that night, and in the morning his sleeping bag was an empty, tousled shell. As it snowed heavily before dawn, there were no tracks.

The men were sorrowful and each man telephoned Helga from the country where he had returned to his wife and children, or partner, or solitary life.

Jan's body remained on the mountain.

Helga later wrote a book gleaning as much information as possible from Jan's climbing companions via email. She noted that they were reticent, and this tugged at her heart. Perhaps there had been conflict? But a Frenchman called Claude, in charge of the expedition, said this had not been the case.

In her book Helga portrayed Claude as a guarded man who undermined the men's psyches. But in her heart she knew that Claude was shy and admirable, where her husband had been hot-headed.

In fact, the evening the news reached her that Jan had wandered from the tent and been slaughtered by the mountain, Helga had not been surprised.

\*

Helga's book became a bestseller in Europe and she gave readings in bookshops all over the continent. In the beginning it was harrowing speaking of Jan's last texts and photos (some had been explicit and she had put these in a secret file), especially when people in the audience asked her did she intend to retrieve her husband's body.

In Copenhagen a journalist asked her about the other climbers, whether she felt rancour towards them and if they had remained in touch. Helga thought of Claude running his abseiling business in the south of France, with his Spanish wife and two daughters. Claude and the other men no longer called her. When approached about Helga's book, Claude had refused to speak to the press.

Helga's publisher wanted a sequel to her book so it was suggested she develop a manuscript about retrieving her husband's body from South America. Jan's body had now been frozen on Aconcagua for five years. Helga hired an assistant, Pieter, to help with her research for the new book. Pieter thought that they would have to enlist at least one of the men from the fatal expedition, to help them retrace Jan's steps that night. In her hotel room in Zurich, Helga wrote emails to all of the other climbers, asking if any of them would join a possible expedition. Helga began to train, hoping she would be able to reach one of the base camps.

None of the other climbers replied.

That summer Claude was killed by lightning in the Pyrenees, and Helga, though it involved an expensive battle with her publisher in court, abandoned her project.

# Tabula Rasa

What Rudy remembered of their last night in Moscow were the gladiators on tables swinging gold-tipped skirts. They had been on vodka and gentle lifts of ecstasy for two days after the boss went back to Milan early, which included the party finale last night. Now they were in the queue at the airport.

Rudy was summarising his thoughts. From the first day he'd felt that he had rejoined a collective of the belly, of the bowels. He'd read the Russians as a youth. You know the feeling when you land in a country and you see them as brethren?

His colleague Leo tapped his arm. 'I wonder what happened to the guy we left at the party,' he said. 'The guy from the hotel who came in the taxi.'

As he fished for his passport, Rudy's mind staggered over the opulence of the party last night. There had been dancing girls entwined with the gladiators, lush girls with ponytails and erupting breasts in gold togas. There had been bodies crammed on balconies embedded in the walls, bodies amassed on stages and crumpling in offshoot rooms. He had never seen anything like it. They had loaded up on vodka before the drugs kicked in. Rudy was good-looking but not a single person hit on him all night; there was only a black guy from Mali in the unisex toilets with whom he sat talking on the floor.

Rudy wondered if he would ever come back here with his job. They were always on the move with their product and usually achieved great success. But here in Moscow they sold nothing, and people had no regard for them. Rudy knew he had flown into the eye of a civilisation where he neither existed nor mattered.

## The Goddess

Max and Marzia were an astounding couple for almost two decades. It was said that Marzia first seduced Max when he was a nineteen-year-old student of Latin, mature for his age. But this was untrue. It was Max who made love to Marzia in a pine-panelled upstairs bedroom of a San Vito mountain lodge, over the *carnevale* weekend. Max had been invited by Marzia's nephew, and Marzia had made a last-minute decision to drive up there to join her older brother's family.

Around this time Marzia was divorced and had not had sex in seven or eight months, mainly because men's genitals made her despair. Her ex-husband, a West African man, had an elegant circumcised organ that she had loved. However, in her home town in northern Italy, Marzia was painfully repelled by the unfamiliar body part otherwise decent men bobbed in her face. She worried she would never fall weightlessly in love again, and would remain governed by the joys she had shared with her ex-husband, an alluring man who had saturated every avenue of her being.

Within the first hour of their intimacy Marzia discovered that the young instrument between Max's thighs was an object she found beautiful and succulent. She enjoyed its scent and vigour, scarcely aware of the young man attached above.

Max looked down upon Marzia's golden hair and the exertions of her profile and saw a goddess, a Diana, a Hera.

The couple emerged from their first night together to a breathtaking meal of eggs and salmon and vodka and caviar recently brought back from Moscow by Marzia's brother. Marzia and Max ate with great appetite and after the meal walked away from their previous lives as though they had emerged from cusps of skin. They skied together all day; Marzia accompanied Max back to his student apartment. Within the week Max had moved into Marzia's place over the river. They were now a sensual, intransigent unit.

Marzia had already experienced the discomfort of the town when she brought home a dark-skinned man with whom she had studied economics in Milan. But this man had found a job in a jazz bar *in centro* and become something of a local personality with his bass guitar and printed shirts. In fact when Marzia came to the bar to introduce Max to her ex-husband, people's views that Marzia was fickle, exuberant and oversexed, were confirmed. It was rumoured that Max and Marzia travelled through Vietnam and Cambodia on a motorbike. It was rumoured that Max stood by Marzia through a breast cancer scare. It was rumoured that he wanted children, but she could not, having contracted some infection in her wayward past. Marzia had been noticed staring at a baby.

*

However, it was Max's wish that their lovemaking should produce no child. His young mind held onto a firm dislike of tugged shirts and toddler food frays, having watched his mother become exasperated and graceless following the arrival of a late, unexpected child. Max said that if Marzia fell pregnant he would have to leave her. He loved her – *God, he loved her!* – but he couldn't allow parenting to strangle this love. Early on he even offered to have a vasectomy, but Marzia couldn't bear the idea of his magnificent virility being extinguished.

Marzia continued to devour Max's organ with its flood of fruit; Max was devoted before Marzia's trim body. But there were many months when Marzia felt that the canal to her womb was the true path towards her being, and that Max had stolen the sustenance of that poor inverted sac. She would cry at those times, feeling toppled and her womanly purpose disputed.

*

Some twenty years passed and one restless humid summer, mid-August, Max left Marzia for a Venetian girl whose very wealthy parents owned an entire palazzo near the Peggy Guggenheim Museum. Previously, Max and Marzia had been to Santorini, sunbathing and hiking, lovemaking and reading, as they did each year. In hindsight Marzia realised that one particular evening, sitting at arm's length on an empty nudist beach listening to the wash and two girls chatting in Greek, Max had been framing his farewell to her.

Newly single, Marzia joined her brother's family in San Vito for the second week of *Ferragosto*, staying in the pine-panelled bedroom where Max had first struggled with her tight jeans and lacy thong. She was not sad. Her brother, who did business in Moscow, kept her plied with vodka and crude jokes. She watched her nephew dress and undress toddlers. She drank a lot, until the watching of small untrained human beings became hilarious, and her brother cupped her shaking shoulders, taking her outside for a chilly walk where she cried and bawled at the sheer, vivid mountain.

*

In April, Max's twins were born. By this time Marzia's own fertility had long been squandered. And yet, despite the wide difference in years, it was Max who quickly grew plump with a crushed, worried face, and was often seen shouting at wailing children in the park. Marzia, while it remained unclear whether it was the yoga retreats or the seeds she was seen buying, or her renewed friendship with the West African ex-husband now managing the jazz bar, grew increasingly superb.

# Life

There were dark, earthen children in the school. The war had ended, and the people had been swept from one end of the country to the other, and now the sombre faces of these new refugee children enclosed riotous teeth. At the nursery school they had crept in, and then there were many.

He leaned on the school fence, making a study of their movements in the playground, wondering whether they were hardier or possessing different skills.

He was ushered away from the school fence by a woman with a whistle.

But he asked her, 'Those dark kids who have come here, are they any different?'

He was a curious man who watched many documentaries, especially about distant places. Perhaps if he had lived in a peaceful country, he might have earned the money to travel. As a man he would have liked to speak to a dark-skinned man, from a village like his own with clambering goats. About his life and his wives (he knew that some tribes allowed several), about the seasons and the soil. Then he would shake this man's hand and know him better.

Earlier in his life the man had raised his two sons after his wife died when her brakes failed on a mountain road. His sons had been active joyful boys. But the war had taken them, and they had not come back.

## A Young Man Reflects

The country where he was born had scorched hills and quixotic animals and wise elders with spectacularly gnarled toes. But it also had knife crimes where there was no mercy and people barbecued dogs, and those elders were diabetic drunkards full of *juju* balderdash.

## A Forty-Nine-Year-Old Woman Sends Messages to Her Thirty-Two-Year-Old Lover

I wait for this love to stop. I wait for the thought of your face and body to mean nothing. I wait to feel droplets for you, not icy waves. I wait to forget your taste, your texture in my mouth, the skin I have savoured. I walk to forget the way you walk, the way you carry yourself, your hesitancy in my eyes, your creeping back, your allegiance to other lives, my smallness, my nothingness, my drama evaporating and bodiless.

## *In God's House*

A feisty woman named Regina almost lost her job with a Christian family stationed in Ghana. What happened was that Regina, five months pregnant (though she claimed it was three), stole a ruffle of notes from Helen's purse and had the baby destroyed in a downtown Accra clinic. The bright girl who prepared Chinese-whisper versions of the Cornish pasty was not only a thief, but she had extinguished a pulsing tangent of Creation.

Eliot, head of the family, brought Regina into the room where his wife Helen made beaded necklaces on her spare mornings. In this house he had no office or elbow space he could call his own.

Regina looked both mournful and expectant, and Eliot knew that she knew this was no time to be deploying her face. Regina's mouth was made prominent by an excess of shimmering teeth and her eyes were crucial and alert. The nub on her belly was gone.

At first Eliot had wanted to drive downtown to the clinic in a fury. Helen, searching for the missing cash for a jaunt to the supermarket, had violated Regina's space and discovered the receipt from a Doctor Lartey in Jamestown. The receipt read: *One Abortion. July 15th.* Long suspecting a hidden pregnancy, what Regina had done had brutally upset the couple. The fact that money from Helen's purse had paid to kill a child! How could they ever make peace with that?

Seven years ago a strong impulse had made Eliot retrain and move his family to West Africa, and it was here that he felt he had access to the unperturbed ruckus of real life. Helen had returned home to Salisbury to give birth to each of their sons, and Eliot largely let go of the stress and digestion ills that had plagued him as a young man, though recently the latter had returned in nocturnal bursts. To date he had no reason to wonder whether his life choice had been rashly crafted.

Eliot sat at Helen's desk with its study lamp and spray of glass beads, each a smoky blue bearing two yellow stripes. A reel of leather cord sat to one side, as well as the bone-handled scissors Helen so often misplaced.

To his right, Regina stood immobile in her work shift, hair swept up in an asymmetrical bouffant. Eliot wondered if they had shown her the corpse, or how the wretched Doctor Lartey had even disposed of this costume of the child's soul.

As expected, Regina stepped forward.

'I will pay you back, Mister Eliot! All of it, I beg!' she said. 'Please don't sack me, Mister Eliot!'

She dropped to her knees on the floor and pressed her hands together like a woman in a triptych.

But now Eliot noticed that Helen's beads were untended and merely strewn there. He realised his wife had been extraordinarily busy of late, that she drifted into the dining room with blazing eyes, that in bed she had become guarded and fitful.

Eliot understood with a monstrous clang that Helen had become another man's creature.

On her knees Regina shuffled over to him. Eliot now saw that it was most often Regina – this murderess – who defused the ever-increasing tantrums of their boys. The young woman laid her perfumed head in Eliot's lap. He felt the weight of her warm skull and knew that this vessel contained the knowledge that Helen would leave him, and the boys, at any moment. What women knew and did – it was they who were the great creators and destroyers. Eliot looked at the comb tracks through Regina's straightened hair.

# Fighters

Corinne Blekker was a busy ambulance worker who had seen many deaths, sheer escapes from death, and not-at-all deaths in her district of Beaune. After work she would come home and lift off her heavy orange coat and hang it in the hallway, and feed her mewing cat before she scooted her out into the tangled yard. If it had been a night shift, she would shower and crawl naked into bed with Matthias, whom she would arouse as he turned and groaned. After all those needles and emergency incisions and oxygen masks making amphibians of elderly faces, Corinne delighted in the robust life of Matthias's member, its disregard for the rest of his grumpy body and the fresh tragedies she saw every night. Corinne was blonde and chesty and an ex-skier, so often, a mildly injured man – say a street fight or a fall down stairs – would interpret her coercive eyes and soothing questions as womanly interest in his person, when it was not.

# In Venice

Donna Carmichael felt the full weight of her name when she and Greg were in Italy. Every time she handed over their passports to a hotel receptionist, the sleek man or abundant woman would show teeth and say 'Donnna! You are a woo-man, Signora Carmichael!' Several hotels into their trip an American explained that *donna* meant 'woman', meaning that Donna's Melbournian parents had christened her with a name that merely flagged her gender.

An amused Greg started calling her Woo-man when they were lying undressed on hotel beds. Greg was a man who almost always invited sex into the room, in ways that were exploratory and tender. But when he called her Woo-man, he encouraged Donna to perform lavish and servile acts.

One glum morning in Venice they climbed back to their room after breakfast, having decided to spend the day in bed. Donna felt tingles of anticipation along the bridge between her legs. They reached the door to their room and Greg inserted the brass key dangling from a burnished ball of wood. They stood looking through the doorway at the rumpled bedsheets they had left an hour ago, the day now reframed.

Greg closed the door. Donna undid her jeans. They stood fondling each other, clothes flying off, until they dropped to the floor and crawled to the centre of the gritty room. Greg breathed the word Woo-man in Donna's eager ear. Something in the muted marine air or beyond the peaked Gothic windows made the game edgier and soon Greg – this was a first – found himself fiercely slapping Donna's rump.

When it was over, Donna rolled on the carpet, her bottom still burning as she returned to the raft of her body. Greg lifted away and went to the bathroom, where he stared at a creeping smile on his face. A boat sloshed past below and Donna looked at Greg's Casanova translation, fallen to the floor.

\*

Donna walked out of the Peggy Guggenheim Museum holding Greg's hand. They were not particularly satisfied; it was an arid, motionless place. What had really stayed with them was something they had seen yesterday in a costume museum. It was a pair of platformed chopines for tiny feet. The woodwork was a chipped sage-green, painted with flowers, and the clogs were impossibly teetering, designed for the high tides that slew through the lagoon town. They were so tall a courtesan would require two maidens to help her walk.

Over drinks Greg and Donna talked about Greg's fierce slapping that morning, and whether they wanted to continue in this vein (or should even), and where it might lead them next. Excited and frank, they looked at the arousing city surrounding them, immersed in the sultry lagoon. Both agreed their urges belonged to a wider carnal history they were keen to plumb.

# Asunder

He parks the rental car at the train station, which is a post-fascist box with marble planes, diminished by concrete extensions on either side. After the unchecked sensuality of the Baroque city he kisses Rachel on the cheek, and she gracefully walks off. He thinks of the sculpted effigies on top of buildings (mostly naked males) and how these posed bodies seemed to be pondering, absorbed by all but the urban fray below. It was sublime what they could do with stone here. It seemed that for centuries men had stared into unhewn blocks and seen glorious bodies to be retrieved.

Rachel, whose Italian is admirable (she studied opera singing but never performed), needs to change their tickets. These are things she likes to do on her own, so he remains in the car park, a recently tarred scallop along the main road, knowing that it may take some time. He knows that Rachel will probably engage the flirtatious ticket officer with his greasy hair, or she might stray into the café for a secret espresso, or get into a conversation with a young mother holding a heavy child.

From where he is parked he observes the tattered wing of the station, seeing how the post-fascist intent lapses into a series of grubby cement alcoves along the final wall. Between this and a railway shed there is a path leading to the platforms, which must have inveigled its way through. A woman in black tights and a bomber jacket walks there now. It seems as though she has no skirt, or the briefest of shorts perhaps at the top of her thighs, or perhaps not.

The woman reverses into one of the alcoves, pulls down her tights as she squats low, and begins to piss. He watches the ripples of her vulva as the spray gushes onto the ground. Her inner thighs are yellow and her parts are violet. Her eyes shoot past him carelessly as she finishes, pulls up her tights and walks away.

He looks around and there is no one but him in the car park. A bus has just passed so the shelter is empty. He switches on the central locking of the car. Right now he cannot remember the face of the young woman, just the rich floral colour between her legs, how he had sat there watching the dab of hair, the gushing water.

Somehow the warm piss has reached him and his hands feel wet. And he's sure that when Rachel comes back she will smell something. Culpability, or a new strand of information she will beg him to surrender, while she leans over inhaling his face.

He will tell her, feeling horrific candour.

But he will never tell Rachel that now this other, vivid aperture will be what he sees always, it will make him faint and bring him to a shocked brink; he will see it every day of his life.

## My Family

He says, *My Family*, and the furthest reaches of your organism, regions that have dwelled in peace within your being as an undiscovered terrain, are incinerated by light.

He says, *My Family*, and you are awash outside a citadel where the walls run into the sky and these are walls that would repel you with a charge, send you smashing across a room.

He says, *My Family*, and you know you have reached your last bastion of hope, and there will be further chains, and no water.

He says, *My Family*, and you remember you were once chaste.

He says, *My Family*, and you imagine the song of their flesh, her cries, his body sweeping, their original compulsion, the shifted radiance, the old radiance.

He says, *My Family*, and you wonder how that pointing of his body felt within the sleeve of yours.

He says, *My Family*, and you remember feeling wishful, all intuition jammed.

# The Vineyard

They were advised to remove the vineyard. The grape trunks had heavy, unruly kinks and were clothed in moss, and the vines that sprang along the wires were each summer weaker and less adorned with fruit. A fast-growing more modern plant was suggested, a hybrid that would show results within three years. It was a soft, easy decision to make given their father had passed last year, so there was no wrath in the room or fists shaken over the table, just the three brothers (Valerio after the car smash had remained slow and staring), one of whom was in the military and mostly concerned with controlling his rebellious daughter, the other was dully married, and the youngest, Maurizio, who as a boy had told unblinking lies but now ably managed the property with his wife Sonia, who was accepting and stifled.

The wires that ran through the grape plants were cut and coiled for further usage. Any plant with additional props had these removed and the concrete posts that rose every three paces were hoisted out of the earth: this took place on a day that Maurizio hired three additional Romanian labourers. When all that was left standing were the rows of limbless grape trunks, Maurizio used his power saw to cut each down, as close as possible to the dirt. The following week he would bring out the digger to overturn the root systems. Then this long job would be half done. The wood gave off a stricken oily odour as he went along.

Maurizio's wife, Sonia, watched his progress from an upper vineyard where she was pruning. These *tocai* plants they always left to the end as they were drier and less prone to sickness, and it was also the most attractive part of the property to work. She stood along an arcade of cropped vines and stopped the compressor for a moment, watching her husband at work. The severed grape trunks were strewn messily in his wake, where Sonia would have told him to stack them to one side. Half the vineyard now lay felled every which way on the wet winter grass. Sonia saw how Maurizio half-knelt with the chainsaw in his lap, and she listened to the whining sound that rose and ceased as he sliced through each one then moved on to the next. She thought of the stash of new green plants in their plastic pockets of fertilised soil, waiting in the barn, how they emanated an unreal eagerness. For a moment she imagined her husband's heartbreak should these young plants fall lifeless to the ground; how he would sit at the table and she would protect him from his critical brothers.

Behind Sonia the sloping vineyard met a stone support wall that harboured snake litters in the summer, and above this a gravel road encircled the rocky hill but led nowhere. Neighbours of hers dumped rubbish there, youngsters buzzed around on motocross bikes, boys stoned cats, and puppies were abandoned.

# *Citrus*

I am holding the baby when he strikes me across the cheek. The house girl pulls back into the kitchen. My sons each become smaller and tighter in their seats. They watch the wake of air as he sweeps from the room. The jeep, on dust, skids across the yard.

I hear pots in the kitchen. I ask the girl to bring oranges. Oranges have solved the crimes of this house.

'We are okay,' I tell the boys. 'We are okay now.'

The boys take their two white plates with two faded oranges before them. They look at the consolation of these spheres. Each inject their oranges with thumbs and lift out the soft stub inside, open up the white pith and the air is citrusy and the yellow skins sit in clumps. The boys are competitive and race to finish first.

In this clammy city there is no power tonight so it was inevitable that we should be this tense. Our small generator sits in the front yard as a swimming squid in an ocean trough, radiating cables to the grimy servants' quarters and this beaten house. The noise flies above with a groggy churning. Our neighbours' houses rest in resilient darkness, charcoal fires and chatter. The palm trees outside have become clacking soldiers.

The baby, now settled again, reaches for my hair, my breast.

The boys' faces sweat as they eat their orange slivers. Everything is fury, everything is rivalry. Their fair hair clings to their foreheads and they glance at each other; one has lost a front tooth.

My boys will become pale, long-limbed men. When they strike their girlfriends and wives, they will smell the citrus of their childhood.

# The Mafia Boss Who Shot
# His Gay Son on a Beach

It was a good day for a killing. The summer had been good. There had been rain, and his arthritis had not bothered him for several months. His wife had gone to her sister in the hills. Elena, his long-time lover, had passed earlier in the afternoon. She had paraded her naked splendour through the house, serving him coffee while he sat in bed. She then moved her nakedness over him.

He had wanted to tell Elena as she cradled his head, the thoughts had been so close to her hands. There had been secrets passed between them before. But Elena had looked down upon his ruined face and told him he was her beauty. He had gazed at her, snakes in his brain, a pit of them.

He had watched the dust scrolls chasing her car.

At sundown he drove into the centre. The bars jostled around the piazza and serene evening light bathed the Basilica facade. He parked his car around the corner and walked to his son's apartment. Upstairs, the balcony shutters were opened wide. His son was at the computer, stroking a cat.

He sat down. What they had told him, he had verified first. But there had been no need. The boy himself had announced his habits. Told him that he liked the Scandinavians who came in the summer or the Africans outside the station. But now they had informed him that his son had begun to deal in the

51

clubs, with his thin addict boyfriend who patrolled the high schools. His son looked at him carefully.

When he asked his son to accompany him to the beach he knew that the boy would inhale. He poured them two glasses of amaro. The young man dressed. They drove north along the coast to a place neither had ever seen, a dull stretch of sand with the water still and green in places. On the rise was a half-built house with girders scratching the air, three date palms spaced unevenly. The young man asked if he might swim. He removed his shirt and trousers, walked into the sea.

The boy later knelt and was shot.

For some time, looking at the way his son's fingers curled into the sand, and strands of seaweed twisted around an unfamiliar ring, the man wondered if he should turn the gun on himself. He put the odorous muzzle into his mouth and took it out again. The sea rushed back and forth. He kicked sand over the body and walked back up to where he had left the car.

As he drove he recalled how Elena's pupils had contracted and he had watched the brown tissue of her irises, which concealed a niche of revulsion. It had aroused him to see the flames surging over this.

# The Height of His Powers

He picked up an Australian girl after the concert. She had caramel hair and an astonishing bottom enhanced – like his own – by years of competitive snowboarding. Before they made love they stood side by side in front of the mirror in his room and both snapped photos of their naked bottoms on their phones. His buttocks were higher and bulkier at the top, with two lateral concaves and a seamless reversion to the thigh. Shinier and softer-looking, hers seemed made of a pearly substance.

The concert had taken place near his apartment in Corvara in the Dolomites, which was across the village from her hotel. He ramped up the fire in the *stufa* and they lay interlocked on the couch, but when this was too cold they transferred to his bunk with its rarely washed covers. Every so often he leapt down to load another piece of wood, then leapt back into the cloud of her body temperature and her enclosing arms. That morning at the races she hadn't even placed in her heats, while he had won all of his and went on to win the finals of his category. At the concert afterwards they had called him up onstage and he took Niko's guitar and played with demonic energy. That is why this girl from the other end of the planet felt like a personal reward entrusted to him. He caressed her neck, demanding to know why he had never laid eyes on her all day. *Where were you? What tree were you hiding behind?* She said laughing that he probably had his eye on some American – the top girl who won, she was pretty hot. He spanked her lightly, turning her over and over to examine the bikini lines dissolved in her tanned southern skin, making her shiver while he tongued his way over these untouched islands. Her hard dark nipples were novel, and he sucked them until she yanked his hair.

The next morning she downed a quick coffee because the bus was coming to collect the team at the hotel. She called ahead as they were waiting for her. She gave him an incomplete kiss and he imagined her sprinting across the village.

He picked up his phone and looked at their two perfect, unassailable bottoms.

*

Around nine his girlfriend in Trieste called to see why his phone had been off all night. He said he'd been completely trashed; then he dangerously added that he'd been getting calls from some random number so he turned his phone off; then he realised he was in the usual quagmire; then he was measuring how much affection or tolerance there might be remaining behind the fury in his girlfriend's voice. He knew that one day she would catapult into the arms of a more decent guy, and then catapult back. It had already happened twice.

He put down the phone, wished to masturbate but his cock was still sore. There were embers in the *stufa*, which he stirred before putting in some sticks which caught alight, then a piece of wood from the pile that had dropped down last night. He thought of the girl with the white triangles on her boobs and her hard-nosed nipple travelling along the roof of his mouth, and how a range of oral exploration had caused no flinching or qualms. He wondered if it were true what she had said when they were comparing notes – that her boyfriend was a bit of a geek who knew she slept around but loved her;

that he was starting up a business and next year wanted her baby.

He imagined some floppy-haired guy entering her on her return, and her marvelling at this guy's face in a bedroom, her snowboard in the garage and the coldness of Europe long forgotten, the photo of their buttocks shown to a girlfriend then snuffed.

# The Last Hike

It was to be their last hike together. They had decided their relationship was over and they were in the kitchen preparing their rucksacks. Family members had been informed that a separation process had begun. Eileen had spoken to two girl-friends about her new lover, Leonard, and Eric had started gathering funds to climb in the Himalayas.

Because there had been no children the house was quiet and tidy, even more so because Eric had been sleeping in a nearby hotel. His blue zippered sports bag lay emptied of dirty clothing on the laundry floor and the washing machine churned around.

'Do you mind if we wait for this to finish so I can hang it out?' Eric said.

'Of course,' said Eileen. 'You're right, I hadn't thought of that.'

So much had been voiced, launched across rooms, accused and muddied. Eric had discovered Eileen sitting upon a man's undone trousers on a garden bench behind the house, her summer dress about her waist. Eric had run up, pushing the bench over onto the concrete path, so that their bodies sprawled and cried out and he was not sure whom his kicks and pummels reached.

The day after he had felt unmanly and childish. The bruised lover had followed Eileen up the path, resting his hand on her shoulder as she rang the doorbell and pleaded to be let inside.

Now Eileen poured a nut mix into two small containers and fastened the lids. She pulled down his old thermos and placed a pair of energy bars on the bench. They would be hiking along a trail that wove in and out of a dramatic waterfall and dropped down into a translucent gorge. Once, many years back, Eileen had been bitten by a snake that lunged out of the leaves. Eric had sliced open the wound and sucked and spat out the venom, carrying her frightened body up the trail to a waiting ambulance and a group of onlookers.

*

That morning in bed, Eileen had reluctantly answered her new lover's intermittent questions about her marriage. Leonard was an older man for whom women left their sturdy husbands, to whom they gave oceans of love. He attracted women who cherished his isolation and distance, his warm hands through their hair and an irreverent roughness. They would batter themselves against his rocky shores.

Leonard had listened to Eileen speaking and remained curious. Several times he had feigned love, but he had never, never reached that blind plateau.

# Banking

A few weeks after Charlotte left her boyfriend she selected a celebratory handbag but discovered her credit card was missing from her purse. Kenneth had been raw, scented and occasionally violent, in a way that had marshalled her into passionate submission. She had finally seen that he was an inconsiderate bully, badly programmed as a child.

She checked online and found that forty-two pounds remained in her account, and the other three thousand had been spent or withdrawn over the past few days. She was livid. This was hard-won holiday money she might have spent with Kenneth on Corfu, clubbing and staying at a beach hotel and drinking cocktails every night. She wouldn't have minded paying for him before, but now she was planning a trip to Norway on the fjords – alone – with her new, non-existent handbag. Did he think she was stupid?

She parked outside his block and pressed his buzzer. No answer. She pressed again, long and relentless, remembering how she used to stand burning right here, how once she had gathered a bag of rose petals from the park and cast these on his bedsheets where they had made spellbinding love.

Kenneth leaned out over the railing, bare-chested, his halo of wild hair cast down. That mane she used to love was now so scrappy.

'Hey, Charlotte.'

'Kenneth, I need to talk.'

'Can't talk.'

'I'm coming up.'

She pulled her body up the stairwell. He let her in. She had already bolted herself up tight so that his lean abdomen and those loose drawstring pants would have no effect upon her. She felt a little undone but thought she was doing fine. Kenneth said he would make her a cup of tea and, although there was no evidence, Charlotte knew the presence of another woman was on display. That noisy woman had been subdued by the magnified, matchless moments of intimacy when she had groaned, like Charlotte, like a cat.

'Did you take my credit card, Kenneth?' Charlotte called out to the kitchenette. 'The money's all gone.'

'What?'

'Give it me.'

'Don't have your credit card, Charlotte.'

He came and sat next to where she was hunched on the couch. Charlotte cupped her hot tea. Kenneth lolled back and his hand reached out, making warm contact with her waist. She felt the journey of his hand, the architecture of the bones, the electric impulses on their travels out from his brain, his bitten-down nails and the bustling transport of his blood.

'Don't touch me,' she said.

She splashed the tea all over him and his grimy couch.

*

Charlotte did not go to Norway. She did not buy the overpriced handbag, inappropriate for a fjord cruise anyway. Kenneth's cries had brought a neighbour running to the front door and rushing inside. Charlotte had never seen this woman before. Much older, with loose clothing, loose breasts, but a firm high rump that stood up challengingly. She looked past Charlotte at Kenneth clutching his stomach. Charlotte was now appalled by what she had done and Kenneth's moans had tapered off.

'Kenneth! What's happened to you?'

Kenneth pulled himself up, retrieved the empty cup Charlotte had tossed at him, told this woman he had been clumsy enough to spill his tea.

'Doreen, Charlotte. Charlotte, Doreen.'

'Hi.'

'Hi.'

Doreen marched out with her firm bottom following close behind. When the door slammed, Charlotte sat there for a full minute. Then her hand crawled over and untied Kenneth's trousers. She got onto her knees and hiked up her dress and steered herself over his cock; gasped at its clean plunging. Their eyes careered into each other.

*

After making love they slept. Leaving Kenneth had truly exhausted Charlotte's body. Her desire and her reason had thrashed together these last weeks; she had lost weight, and her colleagues had become concerned. But now, in the bedroom, enveloped in Kenneth's scent and arms and skin, Charlotte unpicked her rationale. She could easily earn the money again. They would go to Corfu and stay by the beach. She kissed his forehead with its light film of grease after his exertions, marvelling at the way he could drop into slumber the way a bird cruised off a cliff. She wanted to crawl into his dreams.

On the way back from the bathroom Charlotte saw Kenneth's stuffed wallet on a shelf above the bed. It was at eye height, next to another book he had never read, inviting her to rifle through and prove one of them honest, the other thoroughly unjust.

She looked over the composition of their bodies, hers nude and standing, his folded in shades of beauty. She stared at the wallet.

Kenneth's eyes opened.

## The Things You Will Never
## Know About Your Lover

When your lover walks away to the queue at the airport after you've drawn a long hair from his shirt and *this is not the time to cry* has been whispered against your damp neck, a Ute Lemper song flings into your head. 'Little Water Song'. You watch the assembly of his face; the stones are piling on your chest. Cairns and shrines should be made of your dry ribs. What do you know right now, and then before, about this man whose back you have inhaled as though you had given birth to him? Would you even recognise the face he wears over that border, in the worn car and kitchen, in the sedate bedroom with its cries? Would you even recognise the notes in that voice?

He waves and your guesses are so childish.

## The Temperature of Islands

After her heart attack Barbara returned to the island. She knew very well that should anything happen, the helicopter – if available – would take twenty minutes from the mainland. She went straight to the stoned guy on the beach who did winters in India, and bought a purple sarong.

Barbara sunbathed nude. It was heartening – *heartening!* – and her ropey body soon gleamed. Friends passed by. Emmanuel and his poodle-headed partner, Chantal, from Paris. They were already seamed and brown. The northern Italians with their glorious sons. A waddling Greek woman whose rear was a graceful vessel, and whose breasts moved as though they were gourds filled with water.

They all asked her how it had been, this first year without Hervé? Did she have plans to move? Had the children been supportive?

Barbara replied that she had had a heart attack. A smallish one – not at all like the one that had thrown Hervé to the ground when he was sitting at Roula's pouring back raki – but a heart attack nevertheless.

At that her friends remembered the clumsy act of Hervé's dying, the useless propping of his head, the lack of final good-byes, and Roula's extinction of the music. Barbara watched each of them recompose after this.

But—

They wanted to say, But are you not afraid? But the helicopter? Do you not remember that drive to the heliport in the dark? The way those imbeciles had almost tipped Hervé's body onto the rocks?

In fact Barbara did. She smiled at them and rolled over and tanned her bottom.

*

Barbara dragged herself up to the heliport. This was where she had seen the life leaking out of Hervé, vanishing from his furious face. It was true, the paramedics had levered him unevenly so his body almost slid to the ground. One young bearded man had looked at her apologetically. The other had not.

She stood at the rusty chain-wire fence that had been tossed over by the seasons. Growth burst through the concrete slabs, mostly relieved of their coloured paint. This was where she had realised Hervé was leaving her. This was where she saw that life would blaze through each of them, leaving carcasses and flickering shrines. Barbara thought of Hervé the day before, elbow on the table, trying to entice Emmanuel to invest in the faded discothèque on the hill, or at the least hire Manolis's fishing vessel that afternoon – when Hervé knew very well that Emmanuel would never leave Chantal alone on the beach. And then Barbara saw the two of them on their separate beds in the room, each shrouded in greying sheets, Hervé's farts uncontained.

Barbara's heart attack had happened on a train crossing Germany. With discomfort she had stood up to move down the carriage, but found herself wading in water, blind in all but the centre of her eyes, crashing into headrests and shoulders and landing with an injured face in one man's lap. At first they had thought of terrorists, and police charged through looking for youths with knives or guns, until Barbara, whimpering, was surrendered.

Barbara rattled the chain-wire fence. She kicked the metal web. There were wells on the mountain tops with wooden planks laid over the openings, and these were held in place by abrasive stones. There was a temple of loosened rocks with a font made of a burning black substance that Hervé had said was certainly from a meteorite. There was a white church several peaks away where there were candle stubs on a stand upon a powdery square of carpet, and an icon of Saint Gabriel sweeping across a gold frame.

# Slaughter of the Innocents

This is how it goes down. You're at your parents' place out of town in Quinto. Your father leaves the apartment. He leaves the front door unlocked but you don't give a shit because you know what he's done and what he'll do next. You're standing in your knickers holding the dog while your mum is stretched out in her knickers and bra too. You're getting ready to watch TV cos the heat has fucked around with you all day.

That's when they come pounding through the door and you know he's behind this. He was high when he left; he collected all the bottles, dropping them in a carrier bag with your mum screaming *Laisse-les! Laisse-les!* and there they are still sitting on the kitchen floor.

They are six. You smell aggression but you know better than to say a word cos they gave Sandro's sister an anal check when she back-answered in Verona. The creeps told Sandro to take off the scarf wrapping his face and she got dragged away kicking when she said *What the fuck?* Sandro said the bitch's fingers went fucking *deep*.

They turn on lights and dip their heads into all the rooms and want your identity cards which your mum has to rummage for in her bag. She's half-naked standing up pulling out receipts, her boobs jigging in a sort of rage and her pocked thighs and slack arse, and they just stare over her nudity and piled dirty hair.

Now they look at *you*. You are clutching the dog. They have insignias on their shirts which are made of a thicker material, not cotton. This is your last week home here before you trek back to Milan where you are close to moneyless, where you've done some porn stuff with a guy called Luciano whose cock is cartoon-huge.

The dog leaps to the floor and you cover your breasts but for one brown nipple peeping from your arm crook and this is what six pairs of eyes are tonguing and biting hard.

They are saying neighbours called them up cos there were odd lights but this is bullshit; there are no thieves out here. Each one of them has a stitched leather holster nursing a gun.

There's a T-shirt rolled in a ball on the couch so you slide it over your tits, and your mum who was a flawless Tunisian girl with a blessed childhood holds a cushion to her belly. You hate your father more than you love your own life and your skin feels flayed and you know these are the breed of men who can fuck a woman with a bottle or watch on.

They are lingering doing just that, barely containing their combustion, before they march onto the landing, down the stairs and you hear boots crunching gravel in the courtyard. It's all you can do to hold yourself from running to the window and shouting down *Pigs!*

Hours later your dad returns and your mother is still crying in bursts.

# My Thoughts Concerning Letizia

I was told that Letizia was an appropriate type, she was what we wished for. Given you won't supply images I've had to furnish your words. Which can only be called ratty given the level of visual technology at hand. Is Letizia agile? You mentioned she did some sport – was it volleyball or tennis? – I wish you would illuminate. In case you're wondering it's because different muscles are highlighted and given traction – this is something that appears on the screen. This is the arthouse end of a competitive industry, I thought you realised. This is not personal. You will never lose your place. Is that what this is about?

So is there any chance you can get some shots to me? By midday? Or send me her email so I can ask for her portfolio myself? Baby, it's not enough to know that she has an S-shaped body and her shoulders are thrown back, and her breasts are dark-tipped cones. Or that her neck is a little short and she has knock knees that can be hidden initially by a tight skirt. That could all be good material – you've done your homework baby – but her hair, for example, I'm not clear on this. You said it was cropped. Cropped? What does this – for filming purposes – mean? Has it been cut savagely? Will she need a wig? I'm also not reading you with regard to skin tone.

You said she was half-from-somewhere and half-Italian, but what does that mean in terms of lights?

Right now I'm trying to imagine how she moves. You know we require a walking shot along the balcony of the motel. Does she walk well? Does she know how to incorporate her ass into the architecture of her body without seeming like a tramp?

Will you be kind enough to answer me? I'm being kind here. Nothing's at risk. Is it because I refused to rein you in that night, and perhaps it hurt? Okay I made a couple of comments, okay I said what I felt in the moment. But that was encapsulated, it's gone. Baby, just send me the shots. I know you've been working on your own photos – your work is getting stronger all the time and I admire you for it. Look, I've only got the room another day and the guys are on my back, they want their equipment.

Is there something I'm not getting here? Is she so alluring you've taken her for yourself? Well that's okay baby, that's fine baby too. We can write that into the script. You can show me what you've created together and I'll watch, I'll collaborate with you on this. We could film tonight at the motel – any time is good – I'll be waiting for you in the bar downstairs, the guy with the hair transplant and the caipirinha (joking). That's if you have the decency to turn up.

But just fill me in baby. Jesus, I had a feeling it would turn out like this. You and Letizia. It's that name, it spoke to me from the start. Does she know who I am? Don't even dream of thinking you bitches will get away from me.

## On Being Eaten Alive

Two years ago I had a dalliance with a prominent person. A tall, esteemed, white, award-winning author. Obviously I can't name any names. Shall we call him J perhaps?

I queued up to have J's book signed for a girlfriend whose daughter broke her arm that afternoon. Last in the line, dying for a pee, I was contemplating doing a runner and signing the thing myself. At university I had adored J's books but thought he'd become pompous in later life. I had no intention of reading the novel I held in my hands. As the woman in front talked, I imagined her sitting astride J's lap and licking his nostrils. J would be into that sort of thing, I thought, and this kept a patient smile on my face. But then I reached bursting point and rushed off to the toilets.

On the stairway back up to street level, I met J meandering down alone. Initially he looked through me. Then he warmed.

'I'm sorry,' he said. 'You had a book for me to sign.'

Having sat through J's self-absorbed talk, and then watched every crinkle in his face as he listened to the gushing woman, I was bereft of awe.

'Oh, I left it somewhere. I really had to get to the loo.'

J belly-laughed and asked me out for a drink.

*

I didn't fall for him immediately. I am used to a very different sort of man. J was certain of every word that came from his mouth and sometimes seemed to be playing word games with himself, or trying to speak in cadences or chords. In my own life I had decided on music rather than writing (footnote: I am a jazz singer), so J's forays into my world felt clunky. His taste in music was firmly Phil Collins. Sometimes, I had to recall him speaking to an audience of bobbing heads, all eyes feasting upon him, to reboot my fascination.

In bed J was lusty and overt. He would eat me for hours, absolutely entranced and tireless. My orgasms were rich heavens that I could barely clamber down from back into the world. Neither of us had said any words of attachment, and when we made love we did not stare into one another's eyes. But we were kind and chatted daily on the phone (J didn't like texts), even when he was abroad on his book tour he would call and wish me goodnight.

*

The girlfriend whose daughter's arm had been broken that day (who had since bought her own copy of the book, read it and felt unnerved) was at my place one evening and we were getting trashed in my kitchen. J was in New York. Earlier I had sent him my first erotic photo, taken with my phone tilted against a pile of books as I fingered myself on my bed. J was ecstatic. He even called to thank me, just before he had a big interview in a Manhattan hotel. He said he would call me again afterwards, and I told him my friend was here and I'd try not to be too trashed. Then faintly, deftly, almost as an aside, he said, *I love you.*

My girlfriend was just divorced and mopey so the drinks went down fast. She was dating madly online and received text messages every five minutes. She showed me a photo of the primary guy she was seeing, a beautiful Brazilian with a shock of mad hair. *Danger*, I thought, but that's not what I said to her.

By the end of the night all I wanted was for my girlfriend to go home so I could sit around, naked perhaps, and wait for J's phone call. I rang her a taxi and she staggered outside, leaving her car parked in my street. I brushed my teeth and sat nude on my bedcovers, opening my legs and taking invasive photographs of my body which I peered at under the bed lamp.

J did not call.

*

The thing that had unnerved my girlfriend about J's book – this came to me as my mood grew muddier the next morning – was that there had been a new note of intimacy in his work. Charged with being lofty, J had written a love story, one that was teasingly erotic at times. I knew the book had been written before me but I was curious. What if he'd lost the catalyst behind his work, and now sought it through others, and through what everybody wants to read about – sex?

My girlfriend came around in the afternoon to collect her car but she was cranky and still looked a mess. She had to pick up her daughter from hockey, and she and her son had had a fight. She was older than me by eight years and always told me never to have kids. She'd forgotten who she'd loaned J's book to, and what would I care anyhow?

When J flew back to London I expected him to call me up with apologies and announce his need for repose in my arms. I thought of his head parked between my thighs and grew horny. I thought of his cock which I hadn't really liked but had grown used to, even the yelps of his orgasm next to the groans of my own. I thought of the three words whispered from the lobby of a fancy Manhattan hotel.

*

I managed to speak to J once before he changed his number. I caught him when he was in Edinburgh, waiting for a car to pick him up for the festival, so I guess he answered the phone by mistake. He said, *Ah, I see*, when I said I missed him. He said that he'd call as soon as he came back to town. As I said goodbye, there was a gust of relief in his voice.

A while later I heard J in a radio interview saying he was about to 'hunker down' to write a new novel. (He actually used the words hunker down. This is when I realised I had been miles away from falling in love.) The journalist asked – in view of the success of his current novel – a love story for those who hadn't yet read – would he continue to mine this field?

J thought not. In a minor cadence, he mused. 'A thing akin to love,' he said. 'Almost music. Perhaps jazz.'

I knew a lanky Dutch guy called Yannick who played double bass. He was foreign, oblivious to J's prominence. I also knew that J wasn't seeing anyone else and that he really had hunkered down to write his new novel. I had Yannick run into him a few times on the footpath near his house, then recognise him at the local coffee parlour. Yannick dropped the word 'jazz' in their talk, mentioned that he played double bass, and J was in the front seat at Yannick's next concert.

\*

The night of the concert I caught a bus to J's house. I walked up the footpath and slid across the latch of his front gate. I had never been given keys, but I knew the pot plant out the back under which they were hidden. They were not there. I looked under a range of sculpted objects and plant pots but found nothing. I stood before J's back door with its framed glass pane revealing food relics on the broad wooden table where I had once provided the author a carnal meal. The door was ajar a half-inch.

I went straight upstairs to J's office. Not to wreak havoc, but to look over the birthplace of this new novel, the novel that people would read and praise in eighteen months. I looked at the icons J had set up; they were different from the ones that were here a month ago. Sheet music for percussion that I doubted he could read; a print of an older black woman singing in the street, angry-faced. Some arty porn, including stuff that was close to the images I had sent him myself. Next to the open laptop sat a cold cup of J's idea of coffee, but I was not unkind enough to splash it over the keys. Tempted, but no. Through one of our confessionals J had told me that masturbation was a counterweight to his work. He said he needed its cleansing torque. He said that sometimes he would be midway through a reading, and a turn in the text would signify moments when he had been euphoric, when the drag of the words had been given new unthinking vigour, a window fisted through.

I curled up on J's bed. I wanted to do nothing but leave some residue of my body – even a drift of dead cells here on his bedcover, an iron coil of hair – that would pass into the premises of his thoughts. I pulled off my jeans and touched myself. I rocked hard. I left my cries in the air, in every recess of that room, and I slept.

Wandering downstairs afterwards I met J in the hallway, pulling arms out of the flaps of some sort of all-weather jacket. I glided past him and he was transfixed.

# Tokyo Frieze

Tanja and Kurt's story absorbed none of the usual shocks and fractures that beset a union. Tanja and Kurt lived on different continents, in different time zones and contrasting seasons. The few friends who knew what lay behind this panel in their lives believed their rapport to be unrealistically sound, like a creature never saddled or ridden.

It had gone on for ten years now. Meetings in Rome; a week in Bucharest; a few days in Fez; another week outside of Helsinki. Tanja's children were grown and didn't care when she was absent. Kurt had invented a daft seam of conferences and research projects branching from his company work, which his wife might have plucked apart in moments, but did not. He would look over his sons before he left for the airport, visualising a poison tributary through all of them, seeing Tanja as a foreigner upon whom he should never have laid his hands.

If compressing this guilt was difficult, it was even harder to hem off the great pasture of time they might have shared, into counted hours in a hotel room. They often said they suffered the tyranny of these volumes, absolving them through the same anonymity that accused them a thousand times. There was relief and trepidation in their first hugs. A homecoming, a bearing of gifts. Would it be the same? Would love still reside within him/her? Touch was symphonic, placid, brows were smoothed, a nipple mouthed, the unveiled sexual organs already engorged and moist. Sometimes the lovemaking was rushed and instantly completed, while there were other instances imprinted upon both their minds when they had been almost motionless, a maw appearing between them that each had wanted to enter whole, blind to whatever currency had brought them here and a place where both had wanted to die. This had been said. They always spoke freely; he with his accent and she with hers. Perhaps because of the zigzag through languages they were emboldened when addressing each other's eyes.

*

Tanja and Kurt met in Tokyo in the cherry blossom season but never left their room for the first three days. Kurt had been ill. It was an unresolved affliction, and though he hadn't told Tanja, she had guessed. They were on the twenty-seventh floor above Ginza, a harbour of lights. Kurt had said he wished to avoid all the promise in the air, the nectar and straying blossoms, as well as the tourists. Tanja gazed at him, outside it began to rain. Kurt turned on Japanese baseball, and later Tanja read a Murakami story aloud, which left the room airless as the characters joined their thoughts. Tanja walked naked to the kettle and while she waited Kurt watched her form touched by the city light, cusps illuminated on her buttocks and the shadow welling behind, the shiny trail of his spilling traced on her thigh. She made two mugs of green tea. As she walked back to him the light caught on her breasts in the way of Caravaggio, or Georges de la Tour, and Kurt felt his abdomen rustle and every ligament he possessed distend. He declared that he loved her in his language. She placed his tea by his side and nursed his head. Kurt's skin was sheer and polished. Tanja wanted to slide within the bones of his body.

That evening Tanja wanted to go to a jazz club. She told Kurt she wanted to drink a cocktail and perhaps go dancing.

Kurt had outgrown gatherings of people and often played the old man with her. Once, in a club in Athens, he had watched her dance with a youth whose beard became a scrubby collar down his neck. This man had grasped Tanja from behind as Kurt leant on a wall with a sense of this clutch – for he knew the format and cushions of her body. The youth had come home with them. Kurt had watched him possess Tanja, then the pair of them had ridden her until her eyes rolled and she stiffened and howled.

Kurt said he wasn't going anywhere. Tanja showered and zipped up jeans, boots, swung her hair around and combed her ravishing eyebrows upward. Her work took her to intricate places often and alone, and her energy was quixotic and rangy, he knew that in real life they would outpace each other or lag. *Come with me. No. Just take care. I adore you. I do.*

Tanja caught a taxi outside of the hotel to the Roppongi Hill area, to a bar she used to frequent when she was a young woman living in Tokyo with a Japanese man. She had not told Kurt this. Kurt had come through the later chapters of her life. As she sat in the taxi she remembered being within the taut skin of that young woman, how it had felt, what she had eaten, where she had walked in her platform shoes, being lost and then guided along streets by a middle-aged woman or a schoolgirl in a pleated skirt. Once, the Japanese man had brought home a friend from Osaka and the three of them had drunk Tennessee whisky and then fucked together. It had been the very first time Tanja had found herself pinned between two men. She remembered blood that took a week to pass and the men kissing, hands clasping heads, how alarming that beauty had been and it had flooded through her.

She entered the bar and saw it had barely changed. She'd thought it might have been upgraded given the area, but it was quiet and shabby with the same fish tank behind the bar and purple lights. A tattooed woman served drinks with her hair dyed blond, a black arc cutting through it. She ordered a whisky and sat on a stool by the bar. When younger she had felt porous, hyper-human, tied to a common energy or saturation. But now she knew she was confined within the body around her and went no further. Her history was a stream of dioramas like this.

As she sat there a couple of men walked inside. She expected one of them to be her old boyfriend, whom she'd walked out on, into snow.

In all of these years she and Kurt had shared so little of each other. She knew he had three sons and a loving wife who was broad and short with thin sandy hair. He said she'd fallen pregnant the first time they had fumbled together. Tanja had imagined a much younger Kurt spreadeagled in a student dorm, genitals depleted, a *father*. Kurt knew the names of Tanja's daughters and when there had been ghastliness at home he had locked her in his arms. Then they would exult in their possession of one another, and he would break down all the feuds within her.

She knew that Kurt, in Ginza, stood at the glazed window of the hotel room, the city dropping below him.

One of the men who had come in ordered her a fresh drink while she sat there, and it arrived on a frilled pink mat. Soon after the other led her onto the dim platform where couples had begun to dance.

## The Not Sought-After Truth

We would have preferred ignorance, in this case. It's as though you have been harbouring her and she has been eating our flesh. Eating through our fingertips and blackening them with her poison. How many years now? Five or six? You never troubled yourself to think there would be a brutal ending; it is only brutal endings that give pure relief. Not battered agreements or smoothed-out divisions as though on cloth. We're not having any of that. If you ever wanted her locked in your bowels, her fingers extended into you, giving you that disgusting pleasure you deserve, then feed her in her cage, give her more of the scraps and bones she has lived on till now.

Do not tell me this because I am your son. Your truths will dissolve within you, putrid water into soil. I hear the crashing of your implosion and we are clean.

## Ice Lace

Two women ski down a moderate slope hearing the rustle of ice under blades. They have followed arrows pointing right and not left and are headed downward to a terraced bar in the sun, instead of back to the boys' races. There is no turning around unless one continues deeper – down icier slopes – to the slow ski-lift hefting up and across the tabletop of the mountain.

Eleonora unfastens her skis and tramps off to the bathroom. Cinzia removes her gloves and walks onto the deck. An Austrian man meets her eyes as she removes her goggles. Pointed eyes under heavy brows. Empty espresso cup and cigarettes. They don't stare with entitlement in the way Italian men do, they *examine*. Cinzia plonks down (they were up before dawn with the boys), opens her jacket. Sees they are in a pocket on one of the many facets of the uplifted ziggurat of earth, and the view across to the next range is one of pinnacles and lavender glaciers under the clean dome of the sky.

There is oompah-pah music and the waitresses wear embroidered pinafores.

Eleonora wanders over and presses palms to her temples. Her divorcee phase now embraces clubbing with the ski instructors, sex in ski vans and outrageous hangovers.

'You need to drink something.'

'Coffee.'

'Water.'

'We've missed the boys' races then.'

'We have.'

'Shit.'

Cinzia is the friend who assumed the role of big sister during the upheaval of Eleonora's previous year – the discovery of her husband's second family in Romania, including a gabled house in the suburbs of Timișoara and a set of twins, the loss of her delicious health and the suspension of all her interests; her collapse into a perilous stasis. Only lately had Eleonora agreed to come to French cinema night, the Palladian villa excursions and, in August, had brought the boys camping in Croatia with Cinzia's family.

But the skiing, Cinzia shook her head. Eleonora was a natural, powerful skier. The altitude revived her; you could see the dizziness flooding through her limbs, igniting an interior furnace. Last night she'd gone off in jeans and a cropped faux fur jacket. Stacked boots and too much eyeliner. She'd looked defiant, angelic, awesome.

Cinzia strokes Eleonora's hair, waits for the coffee to take hold. Sees her biting a young man's neck, touching his high flanks and the valley of his spine.

# Trionfo di Pesce

Helen and Marco are celebrating their second wedding anniversary with a joint outing to the new Italian fish restaurant. Marco, whose parents sailed out to Australia from Puglia, orders *trionfo di pesce*, an extravagant mixed platter. At fifty-four, unmarried, Marco had flown to Sydney to visit his brother, when at an inner-city bus stop he met Helen, a childless librarian. Now the couple is living in West Africa until Marco's contract runs out. Opposite them sit their friends, Megan and Geoff, who have been married thirty-four years.

Helen and Marco have not yet mastered the art of being touchy in front of other people. Helen's hands become faltering appendages, and Marco's arms feel like unbending steel rods. So they refrain from closeness in public, although Marco touches Helen's hand when the waitress waltzes away with their order and returns with a tray of thin-stemmed glasses. Helen looks at their clutching digits.

Geoff is given the wine to taste. His quiff of ragged grey hair makes him seem head of the table.

Marco is bald.

One of Geoff and Megan's four daughters has just been involved in a drug-related incident where she fell from a first-floor balcony onto a pool deck. Days ago Megan flew in from Brisbane, assured that there would be no long-term spinal damage. Megan apologises for being a bit teary, and Geoff's large arm swings around her shoulders, patting her upper sleeve.

Helen looks beyond their heads to other couples, other groups of diners, then through the window with its flourished security grill, to a local man leaning on the balcony railing outside. At first it had felt extraordinary to be a man's wife, but she found so much conversation draining.

Marco refills everyone's glasses, remarking that the wine was a pretty good choice.

'So how does it feel then? Two years of marriage?' Megan says, nudging Greg's round abdomen. 'They're just babes in the woods.'

Marco looks at Helen; they were still reading each other's looks.

'Wonderful,' she replies. 'He's just short of being a saint.' Helen genuinely believes this. Marco brings her a cup of tea in bed in the morning. She doesn't always like his nuzzling, but tries to. Helen is fierce-looking with long coarse blond-grey hair and has never much been interested in men, or women. But Marco had struck her; he was only in Sydney for two weeks.

She and Marco have a dream for when they leave West Africa. A little stone terrace in Puglia, the one he'd shown her that had belonged to his grandparents, in a village by the lapping sea. They have both saved their money. They both like to fish. Helen knows that as he ages, Marco will chatter less and he will teach her Italian. That in the afternoons he will fall into a serene silence in the sunlight.

In the car park the couples hug goodbye and Geoff's arm gathers Megan's shoulders. Helen and Marco stand side by side.

Inside the car Helen kisses him and kisses him.

# The Woman Who Previously Worked for the Louvre

It took them two years to find the house and in those two years their rapport nearly overturned. Arnaud, who kept the studio in Marseilles, began working closely with a set designer who drove over from Nice early every morning in a white van. Marianne developed rheumatoid arthritis in both hands, and these became unseemly paws wrapped in flaming skin.

When the house initially presented itself, they were not aware that it coincided with the many conditions they had listed with the young agent, who rolled her eyes every time she saw Marianne's number appear on her cell phone. A bulky house in a cul-de-sac, it stood on a rough sloping block at a distance from a village. It was recently built and charmless. Marianne checked the address the woman had given them, as the woman had been called away to tend an ill child. Arnaud, a patient southerner, looked at the oleander trees rubbing against a mouldy yellow wall.

'She can't be serious. Who would live out here?'

Marianne, since her illness began, had come to believe that other people's lives were less complex, while worrying that her own life would go unrecognised. For so many years she had grappled with creative projects that had flatlined, leaving her urges gathered on a precipice. Rarely had she felt the true satisfaction of a work in flight and acclaimed at the same time. So many things came down to timing.

On the other hand, Arnaud, to whom she had returned after fifteen months with a Dutch saxophonist, had always worked with lucid, committed rashness. His ideas fell open on a sketch pad, then, with the help of his assistants, were transposed into scale models. Over months these structures grew into theatre sets that were the bold embodiment of his art. He was fidgety and silent at each stage of this voluptuous trajectory. In Addis Ababa, Marianne had watched Arnaud attach a paintbrush to a long wooden rod with a coil of wire, and spend the hours colouring wooden set pieces in poor light. This was the most lyrical scene of her life.

But they were considering their retirement now. Arnaud would collect a meaningful pension from the state for his many collaborations. Marianne, who had taught begrudgingly at a Paris high school, could only expect a pittance. Arnaud shook out one of the many filterless Celtiques cigarettes that kept him alive as much as killed him.

'What a foolish woman!' Marianne said again, starting to trot back to the car.

But Arnaud paused at the gate for a very sound reason. There was a sticker with the emblem of the Louvre Museum next to the metal letterbox. He had heard of a woman who lived out here, somewhere in the south, a woman who restored paintings for the great museum. He'd been told there was a slot at the back of a house through which more than one monumental Delacroix had passed. A house where Courbet and Manet had been examined and, without supervision, repaired. The light inside could only have been astonishing.

'Wait, Marianne,' he said. 'Wait up, my flower.'

Marianne turned around. Arnaud's hair, always stringy, fell to one side. In all seasons he wore a navy mandarin jacket whenever he ventured beyond the high-ceilinged studio they still owned in Rue Paradis, even into the cobbled courtyard where he toed out his cigarettes. Arnaud asked her for the keys they had been given, and she followed him through the gate.

Inside the garden walls shrubs lunged at them. The house had been vacant for four years. The woman who lived there was Belgian and she had sold up, no reason was given. Marianne, who had never trimmed a plant in her life, felt a rush of interest in greenery, sensing its embrace.

'Don't touch those,' said Arnaud as she fondled the bank of oleander. 'Not good.'

Marianne had raw swollen hands anyway.

Arnaud skirted the side of the building, and Marianne asked what he was looking for. Couldn't they just go through the front door? He told her about this legendary woman, and how he was certain this was the house where she had lived, that there had to be an entry passage where the great paintings were slotted through.

And there it was. In the middle of the southern-facing back wall, an elongated vertical sliver had been cut through the stucco, in between an arrangement of windows. It looked like a device for warfare perhaps, and was full of cobwebs and dry leaves. Arnaud picked up a fallen branch on the ground and poked inside. Of course it was sealed off.

From where she was standing Marianne saw the village clutching a nearby hill, in placid morning light. She knew this particular village quite well, as they had lodged there with some Armenian colleagues of Arnaud, for the pre-production phase of a project he later told her had been stifling, though no one could have guessed. The only woman in the house, she had gone for walks in the afternoons when she grew tired of their smoky philosophising. She remembered there was a trail all the way over to this side of the valley, then back to the square where the church bell had just begun its faint ringing.

She felt a drag in her belly, a wanting to pee but a sexual spasm as well; she'd grown confused about the unreliable signals that climbed up from there.

Arnaud was hauling himself up the back stairs to the shallow porch crossing the facade halfway. It looked like there was room for a table and chairs, and that an awning had been torn off by wind. His hands were cupped against the glass.

Marianne stood on the ground firmly, inhaling lavender and thyme. She was certain she would say *no* initially; there was a colossal amount of work to do, and much expense. It would be ridiculous to live so far from friends, from the city they knew and loved, but what did friends and a city really mean to one? Who amongst their friends could help them understand the interval that lay between them and their deaths?

Arnaud found the back door key in the batch and they entered. They'd been given no idea of the floor plan so what they found inside was a surprise. Apart from the narrow kitchen space at the head of the stairs, the main floor was a cavernous space. There was a sitting area evident by the windows overlooking the landscape, but behind this the studio immediately expanded into a glowing vault that lifted all the way to the roof. Broad sky lighting had been installed, though one window was unhappily smashed, while to the rear a balustrade at the first floor level showed a series of bedroom and bathroom doors.

Arnaud walked up to the fissure in the wall which began at knee height and travelled upward. This was where the paintings had been passed through to the Belgian restorer, who had unveiled them here, beneath this mantle of light. Arnaud had long been inspired by the immense tableaux of the classicists with their heavy-shouldered women brandishing flags, or their bulbous post-rape bodies crumpled with foreshortening.

# Welcome Home, Moira!

With no warning at all Moira was back in Sydney on our front doorstep. She'd been away in Asia for two years, travelling through India and Vietnam and Cambodia with her boyfriend. Then her boyfriend – she'd met him along the way – had been held up and kidnapped and his body found down a ravine. Moira had helped with investigations, singling out the murderer, who was hanged. At the time she told our parents that she wasn't coming home, perhaps *ever!* And yet here she was.

Moira sank into the living room sofa once our parents were through hugging her. Then she pulled herself up straight and asked for me. She held her arms around me, and they were weightless strings. She smelt of dirt, of clothes at the bottom of the laundry basket, of oily hair. When her face pulled away, her nose seemed enlarged, although her face had become etched and tightened.

Our parents owned a pizza place and hurried off to work.

I asked Moira if she wanted tea.

I noticed that not a tear had been shed.

Before Moira left she was studying to be a doctor. She said she wanted to work in Africa, to help women who died in childbirth. Her goal was to work with *Médecins Sans Frontières*. But halfway through her course she dropped out and began to work three jobs. She left. With Moira's departure

I became the central child, upon whom my parents' hopes were placed. I studied hard, remained a virgin, decided that I would enrol in engineering. When I finished high school my parents paid for a trip to Italy where I stayed with Sicilian relations, who sent me home like a fattened, deflowered pig.

Moira's murdered boyfriend had been Canadian. He had come from a town far far in the north and his remains had been sent home to be buried.

I sat down opposite Moira. We both held our mugs of tea. I asked her if she was hungry and she said she had eaten, that in truth she had arrived a few days back and been staying with friends. She looked around the room where she had become largely absent, and remained so even as she sat there and breathed.

## A Woman Told Me This

A woman told me this: when her lover died she went to the church and sat in the second-to-last pew, where she knew she would attract little attention for they had been colleagues for a stretch. At the front of the church stood the man's wife with her shredded curls, and the two sons whose foibles and brushes with the law and opulent tattoos she knew as intimately as those of the children she'd never had. Did she feel robbed of a life? He had told her that she would. That one day it would seize up inside of her, the wish to uproot all he had ever planted in her, every gasp and cell and flourish of his liquid and the burning of her skin and parts. He had told her she would want to eviscerate her own bowels to be emptied of him, and remove her heart from its safe cage like a wild native, splashing it to the ground with its torn tubes. Her lover had been a dramatic, vital man who liked to toy with their darkest entwined currents, especially as he stroked her hair in bed, or his knuckles drew across her belly.

The woman told me these things, adding that the embrace of this man was the only thing she would take from this earth.

## *Love Is an Infinite Victory*

They decided to rent out the farmhouse to the daughter of their best friends. The young woman had been a charming, mischievous child always twisted around her mother's legs, and had studied agriculture before moving away to Jordan to work on irrigation projects. She and her Jordanian husband were now expecting their first child.

As best as they could, they removed mementos and personal artefacts from the rooms, using their son's upstairs study to store crates that were sealed just in case. Photo albums, treasured books, favourite kitchenware and artwork, along with both of their slim wardrobes, went into these wooden boxes. At first the husband had wanted to put them in a disused shed on the property, but they decided their effects might more likely be prone to fire, damp or theft.

They handed over the keys to the slight young woman with her swollen belly just beginning the show under her dress, and the handsome man with thick waves of black hair and erudite glasses. They felt reassured in the face of such purity, that their house would be looked after and loved.

*

They moved back to Paris where they had begun their lives together many years ago, feeling denuded and carefree as students. They had always kept this tiny apartment, and it was a good thing too. When their own son was at university he had stayed here, and it had served through the periods when their marriage had been strained, when either had gone there to breathe and revive, sometimes taking lovers there to fuck and discard, for they were bound to one another.

Free of decor, with its squeaky herringbone wooden floors and small rooms, the apartment showed no record of their lives, so they were as guests. They resumed heady, unsophisticated lovemaking on the mattress their son had left there, especially through the long mornings when the city revolved and banged and wailed around them. The man found that his erections were sturdy and ongoing; the woman's parts were bathed and her breasts heaved in fiery peaks.

They were so grateful for this, crooning into necks and crevasses. They had not expected this rising.

In the afternoons the man wrote his articles and the woman strolled in the park, or all the way to the river from where she would call him, describing people or birds.

*

Halfway through the summer the young Jordanian husband called the mobile phone that the older man had left on the kitchen counter. He and his wife were in bed together and the call was ignored. That afternoon the young man called again.

He said that his wife had lost the baby – the tiny girl had died inside of her – and they wished to leave the farmhouse. He said that his wife was broken and they could stay in that place no longer. She was coming home from the hospital tomorrow and they would return to the city. He was presently sleeping in a hotel.

He said they wanted no refund for the rent they had paid, just to be away from there. If there was a place they could leave the keys?

*Of course*, said the older man. *I am so sorry—*

The call ended and the man resumed his work. When it was complete, he walked through the rooms of the apartment with its blank walls, and on one of the walls he placed his open palms and leaned his body weight and dropped his head. There were piles of clothing on chairs and cleaning implements grouped in a corner. He thought of the empty farmhouse with its verdant summer growth, the bird calls that rang out after dark and his wife's slumbering beside him, how there were nights when there was a quickened tampering in his heart and he would go downstairs onto the terrace, feel the warm drifts from the woods like the hands that would take him.

# ACKNOWLEDGEMENTS

Thank you to the hard-working editors of the journals where these stories were first published. Immense thanks to Giacomo Piussi for the brilliant cover image, and to Daniele Francesco Fona for the great cover art work. Thanks to Michael Loveday, Christopher James, Michelle Elvy, Ken Elkes, Abha Iyengar, Eric Akoto, Lana Citron and Rachael Smart for their generous comments. Thanks to Gregory Papadogiannis of Eyelands Publishing for my time writing in Athens and also at the Three Rock Studio, Crete. Thanks to my agent Imogen Pelham. Thanks to Eric Akoto and the team at *Litro* where I love my job as Flash Friday Editor. Very grateful to David Borrowdale of Reflex Press for believing in this collection.

\*

The author and publisher wish to thank the editors of the journals in which the following stories were published:

'As Simple As Water' was first published in *The Collagist* (now *The Rupture*), August 2016; 'Foundation Song' – *Sonder Magazine*, August 2016; 'Genitalia' – *Ambit*, July 2016; 'The Woman Whose Husband Died in a Climbing Accident' – *The Collagist* (now *The Rupture*), August 2016; 'Tabula Rasa' – *Reflex Fiction*, April 2017; 'The Goddess' – *Spelk*, July 2017; 'A Young Man Reflects' – *Literary Orphans*, July 2016; 'Life'

– *Flash Frontier*, June 2016; 'A Forty-Nine-Year-Old Woman Sends Messages to Her Thirty-Two-Year-Old Lover' – *Micro Madness*, June 2016; 'In God's House' – *Lakeview Journal*, August 2016; 'Fighters' – *Sonder Magazine*, August 2016; 'Asunder' – *Broadside Series, Blue Five Notebook*, February 2017; 'My Family' – *Sonder Magazine*, August 2016; 'The Vineyard' – *A Box of Stars Under the Bed, National Flash Fiction Day Anthology*, June 2016; 'Citrus' – *FlashFlood Blog, National Flash Fiction Day 164*, June 2016; 'The Mafia Boss Who Shot His Son on a Beach' – *Flash Fiction Magazine*, September 2016; 'The Height of His Powers' – *Wigleaf*, August 2017; 'The Last Hike' – *Spelk*, February 2017; 'Banking' – *Strands Lit Sphere*, October 2016; 'The Things That You Will Never Know About Your Lover' – *The Creative Process*, June 2017; 'The Temperature of Islands' – *Lunch Ticket*, December 2017; 'Slaughter of the Innocents' – *Jellyfish Review*, October 2017; 'My Thoughts Concerning Letizia' – *Moonpark Review*, July 2017; 'On Being Eaten Alive' – *Fiction Pool*, December 2016, and *The Amorist*, July 2017; 'Tokyo Frieze' – *The Amorist*, November 2017; 'The Not Sought-After Truth' – *The Creative Process*, June 2017; 'Trionfo di Pesce' – *Jellyfish Review*, March 2017; 'The Woman Who Previously Worked in the Louvre' – *Connotations*, May 2017; 'A Woman Told Me This' – *Vestal Review*, February 2017; 'Love Is an Infinite Victory' – *Ellipsis Zine*, November 2017, and *Flash Frontier*, April 2019.

OTHER TITLES FROM REFLEX PRESS

## *Some Days Are Better Than Ours*
### Barbara Byar

*Some Days Are Better Than Ours* is a startling collection that explores human life in all its forms. These stories will make you draw breath as you race through compelling accounts of the dark places people escape to and from.

Through her masterful use of language, Barbara Byar skilfully invites the reader into imagined futures and regretful pasts – from war to childhood to road trips to relationships. Her pieces are visceral, sometimes brutal but sliced through with hope. These stories, and the characters in them, strike straight at the realist heart of the human experience and will linger long after reading.

*'These are searingly truthful fictions. Pitched at the border of poetry and prose, they catalogue lives lived at the edge, survivors facing the beauty and cruelty of the world. These fictions will take your breath away.'*
—William Wall, *Suzy Suzy* and *Grace's Day*

*'Barbara Byar writes flash like no one else; in each of these lucid and furious twenty-nine stories – some no longer than a single page – are wholly unforgettable glimpses into the lives of her individual characters.'*
—Peter Jordan, *Calls to Distant Places*

# Families and Other Natural Disasters
## Anita Goveas

*Families and Other Natural Disasters* is a collection of flash fiction about families, born into, created or found, how they support us or repress us, and the ways they can change us and shape us.

These stories are set in the UK and India, in aquariums, ballrooms and outer space. They follow women into volcanoes and out to sea. The characters search for lost brothers and lost selves and find prairie dogs and sea serpents.

In a debut collection rich in cultural detail, Anita Goveas beautifully explores the theme of family as one of the essential elements that hold the universe together.

*'Narratives that intersect continents, myths and folklore – a magical exploration of love, belief and the complications in relationships, with others and with oneself. Left me breathless and craving for more.'*

—Susmita Bhattacharya,
*The Normal State of Mind* and *Table Manners*

*'This gorgeous collection brims with energy and sensuality. Richly observed stories to catch the heart and quicken the pulse.'*

—Sharon Telfer,
two-time winner of the Bath Flash Fiction Award

# *Where Oceans Meet*
## Heather McQuillan

*Where Oceans Meet* is a collection of sixty-one flash fiction stories from award-winning New Zealand writer Heather McQuillan.

Though small, the stories in *Where Oceans Meet* are substantial, often moving, and impressive in their employment of detail. They bring to the page varied perspectives and diverse aesthetics from a realism to surrealism.

These are stories in which characters yearn for connection but sometimes find, as in the title story, that 'when the vectors of the oceans' wave fronts meet at an angle, sometimes they cancel each other, sometimes they compound with spectacular results'.

*'Deeply absorbing, these stories creep under your skin with their pressing sense of longing.'*
—Michelle Elvy, *the everrumble*

*'Read some of the finest flash fiction to enter the universe in Heather McQuillan's Where Oceans Meet. Each of the tiny stories in this collection is beautifully crafted with sentences that can induce physical changes in the body, from tears to a somersaulting stomach.'*
—Nod Ghosh, *Filthy Sucre* and *The Crazed Wind*

## *Witches Sail in Eggshells*
### Chloe Turner

'Witches sail in eggshells,' I heard Meg say from behind me, and I looked back. She was pounding the shells, hard, with the palm of her hand on the flat of a knife.

Perceptive, intriguing, and beautifully told, Chloe Turner's debut collection explores the themes of love, loss, the little ways we let each other down, and how we can find each other again.

*'I adored this collection and know that it will take pride of place on my bookshelf. I am extremely excited to read more of Chloe Turner's work.'*

—Bookish Chat

*'It's been a while since I've read short stories which affected me so much. Never have I laughed, shivered and gawped so much. With Witches Sail in Eggshells Chloe Turner has made me look at short stories in a different way.'*

—The Bobsphere

REFLEX PRESS

Reflex Press is an independent publisher based in Abingdon, Oxfordshire, committed to publishing bold and innovative books by emerging authors from across the UK and beyond.

Since our inception in 2018, we have published award-winning short story collections, flash fiction anthologies, and novella-length fiction.

**www.reflex.press**
**@reflexfiction**